ABC'S OF OUR SPIRITUAL CONNECTION

Written and Illustrated by

KIM SOO GOODTRACK

Canadian Cataloguing in Publication Data
 Goodtrack, Kim Soo, 1955–
 ABC's of our spiritual connection

 ISBN 0-919441-44-0
 1. Indians of North America–Religion and
mythology–Juvenile literature. 2. Alphabet–
Juvenile literature. I. Title.
E98.R3G65 1993   j299'.72   C93-091944-0

THEYTUS BOOKS
Post Office Box 20040
Penticton, British Columbia
Canada V2A 8K3

Design: Susan Fergusson

The publishers acknowledge the support of the Canada Council and the Cultural Services Branch of the Province of British Columbia in the publication of this book.

Printed in Hong Kong by Wing King Tong

ABC'S OF OUR SPIRITUAL CONNECTION

Throughout North America, First Nations People have many common bonds. In this ABC book I have shown our Traditional Values accompanied with contemporary concepts. These values are held by all First Nations People. We have so much to share and be proud of. Our Spiritual connection was shamed and denied, yet it has survived. Here is a collaboration of First Nations Ethics. I hope you enjoy them and respect them.

Kim Soo Goodtrack

This ABC book is dedicated to all the First Nations' sacred ceremonies and beliefs that are not mentioned here. It is also for Dana, Don and Ronnie, my grandmother Pearl and all children on Mother Earth.

Kim Soo Goodtrack

Aa is for All My Relations.

This means our spiritual connection to everything that is part of creation. The animal family, birds, trees, flowers and each other. We are all brothers and sisters ... You are my Brother, and You are my Sister.

arrow heads   antlers   arrow
Aboriginal child   ABC book

Bb is for braid, a sweetgrass braid.

We use this to pray with. We wash in the smoke to help us live by good values. There are 21 blades of grass, each standing for a lesson in life. We all have a variation of this purification ceremony, but different plants ... Cedar, Juniper, Tobacco, Sage.

beaded belts   bent box   baskets

bells   bones   button blanket   berries

ball   bannock   bow   beaded bag

Cc is for Creator.

When we pray we ask for guidance and to be a good person. Creator is the maker of all. We have many different prayers, they vary from region to region, Nation to Nation.

Cowichan   canoes   cedar   clay   containers
Chief's headdress   corn   clams

Dd is for the drum, the heart beat of Mother Earth.

Some drums originated from animal skins while others were wooden planks. They are used in ceremonies and for singing at Pow Wows. The beat and the songs vary from Nation to Nation. There are 45 First Nations Doctors in Canada. They make us feel better when we are sick.

dreaming   deer   drum stick
doe skin   dress   Doctor

Ee is for Eagle.

We respect the eagle so much. The Eagle is part of Creation, and we honour their presence. Eagle feathers are given to people that are doing good deeds and are rewarded with a feather. In some Nations Eagle down is sprinkled at weddings and special ceremonies for peace and goodwill. Eagle bone whistle is also very special to many of us. When you see a flying Eagle say a little prayer.

Eagle   earring   soaring Eagle
Eagle feather   Eagle down

Ff is for Feast.

All First Nations have gatherings for different celebrations. At Give Aways and Potlatches many things are given away... food, blankets, sugar, flour, towels and much more. At Feasts there's lots of food! We were the first farmers in North America. Every season we stored our seeds, planted them and harvested the crop. Each season brought thankful ceremonies.

fish   featherfan   fire
feast   farmer   flour

Gg is for Great Spirit.

Our Creator. Each First Nation has their own way of saying Great Spirit, in their own language. The Grass dancer celebrates the prairie grass that the buffalo ate. The buffalo were very important staple in the central part of North America.

games   grease bowl   guitarist
Grass Dancer   Great Spirit

Hh is for headdress.

Just as each First Nation is distinct so are our hats and head pieces. They differ from region to region. The materials used in making them also vary. The Haida hat has a weave so tight, that it is waterproof. The roach is made from porcupine hair. Eagle feathers are used in many headdresses across North America. Wearing an Eagle feather headdress is considered an honour. The hoop dance is a "Plains" dance. The Hoop Dancers are skilled in maneuvering the hoops up and down their bodies while dancing to the beat of the drum. The Hoop has many Spiritual meanings... The Sacred Circle of life. You might see a Hoop Dancer at a Powwow if you're lucky!

hair ties   hats   hair barrettes
hoops   headdresses   Hoop Dancer

Ii is for Inuit.

The Inuit people are distinct from their fellow southern First Nations Brothers and Sisters. Distinct in their language, art, culture, and Traditions. The Inuit Nation stretches from Alaska, Northwest Territories to Labrador. Inuit Art is world renowned and world class. The carving of rock has been passed down from generation to generation. Have you ever seen an Inuit Carving?

Jj is for jingle dress.

Traditionally, the jingles were made of shells, or deer hooves. Today, we use metal bells. The sound of the jingles when a woman dances is magical! At Powwows when there's a jingle dance all the women whom have jingle dresses on dance together. Dancing to the singing and drum, the women move with grace. The collective sound is very enriching. The jingle dress is a bit heavy to wear! We have so many different types of jewellery. Each Nation has unique materials that they use to create beautiful necklaces, earrings, and rings.

Juniper Smudging   jingle dress
jewellery   jade

Kk is for kayak.

The kayak is a one person small covered canoe. When you're paddling in the water you can tip over and correct yourself by flipping upright. They are very safe. The kayak originated in the North. The Inuit use them for hunting.

The Killerwhale is a "Westcoast" source of many legends. It is also the name of a clan. Many artists carve the Killerwhale in wood, totems, silver and gold.

kelp   Killerwhale   kayak

Ll is for Love...

Motherly love, Fatherly love, Creator's love, Sisterly love, Brotherly love and loving yourself. That's what love is all about. Nurture it, give it freely, surround yourself with love and Pray for a Good life for all... we deserve it!!

The Long House is also regional and diverse. Not only are they homes they're a way of governing. "Westcoast" and "Six Nations" have Long Houses.

First Nations Lawyers are very important for working within the laws of Canada to help protect our existing rights and our future rights.

leather   Long Houses   love   lawyer

Mm is for Medicine Wheel.

The sacred circle of life. Many First Nations have the Sacred Circle. The cycle of life, four directions, the four races, the keepers of fire, water, air, and earth are all intricate elements of the Medicine Wheel.

Manitu is how the Saulteau Nation pronounce Creator.

We have our own Medicine and our own healing methods, in every First Nation. Aspirin is derived from Willow which is found in many of our Medicine bags.

moon   Manitu   Medicine bag
moccasins   Medicine Wheel

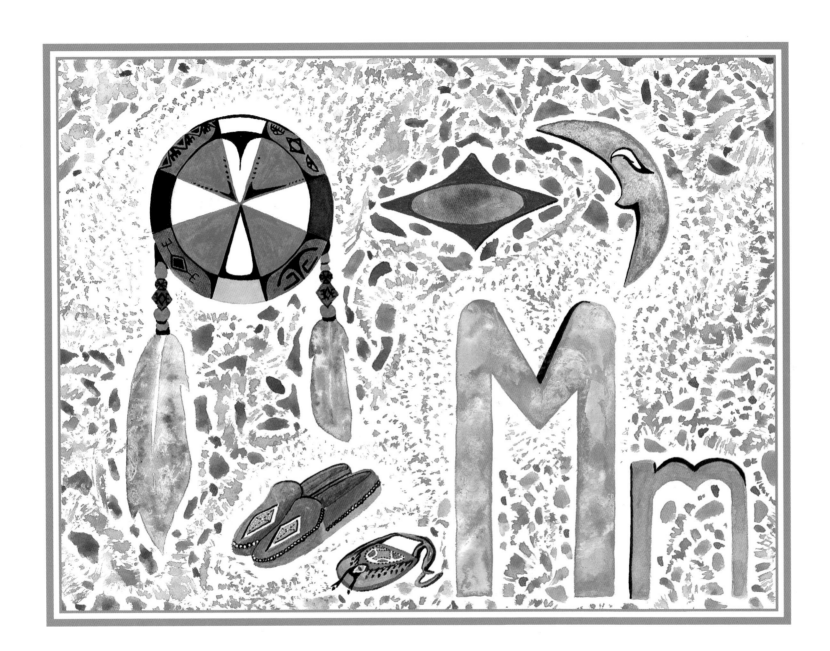

Nn is for Nature.

The respect we have for Nature is part of the underlying essence of being First Nations. We are the keeper's of Mother Earth. A genuine respect for the fragile balance of nature is part of the "Old Way" and today's way. The traditional history of how we respect everything that is on Mother Earth connects all First Nations.

Oo is for Ogopogo!

The Okanagan First Nation's People were the first to see Ogopogo!! "Oh, oh, here's trouble!" You'd better hold on to the side of the canoe!! There he gooooooooooooes!

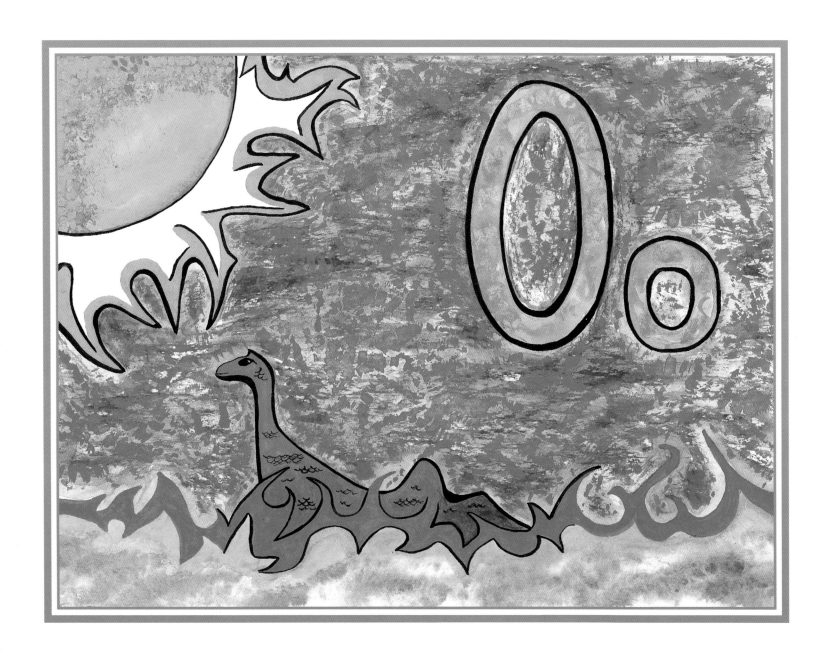

Pp is for Sacred Pipe and Praying.

The passing of a Sacred Pipe around a circle of people is a "Plains" tradition. Sharing a Sacred Pipe brings us together in a Peaceful way. Sometimes we don't puff on it, instead, we press it to our heart and hold good thoughts.

Praying is very important to all First Nation's People. Some of us pray when we pick something to eat from Mother Earth. We all have wedding Prayers and Birth Prayers. We have Thankful Prayers for the Plentifulness on Mother Earth. We have many Prayers in many different First Nation's languages.

pumpkin   pemmican   potatoes

Sacred Pipe   praying

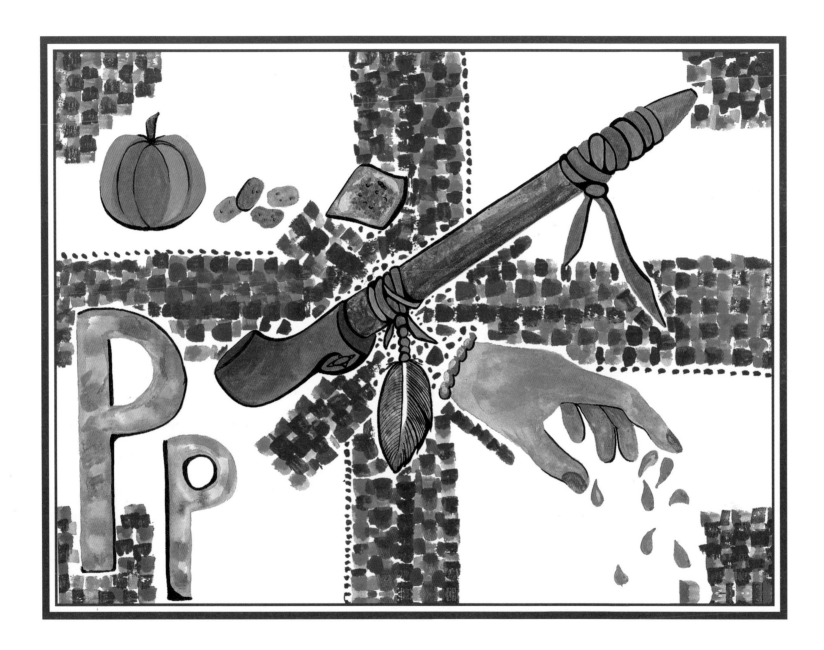

**Qq** **is for Quill basket.**

Porcupine quills are used in many intricate creations and patterns. Quills are used in making earrings, baskets and, the designs on bags and moccasins.
Star quilts made today often have a story accompanying them.

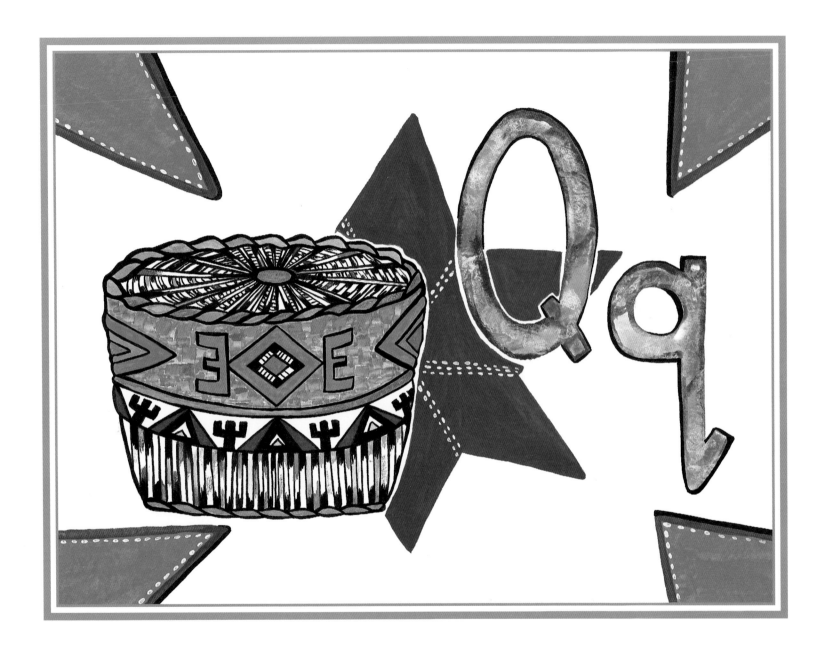

Rr is for Raven Rattle.

The rattle is used from coast to coast by First Nation's People that are on the Spiritual Path in life. The materials that are used in making rattles vary greatly from Nation to Nation. This is a "Northwest Coast" cedar rattle.

rope   rugs   rattles

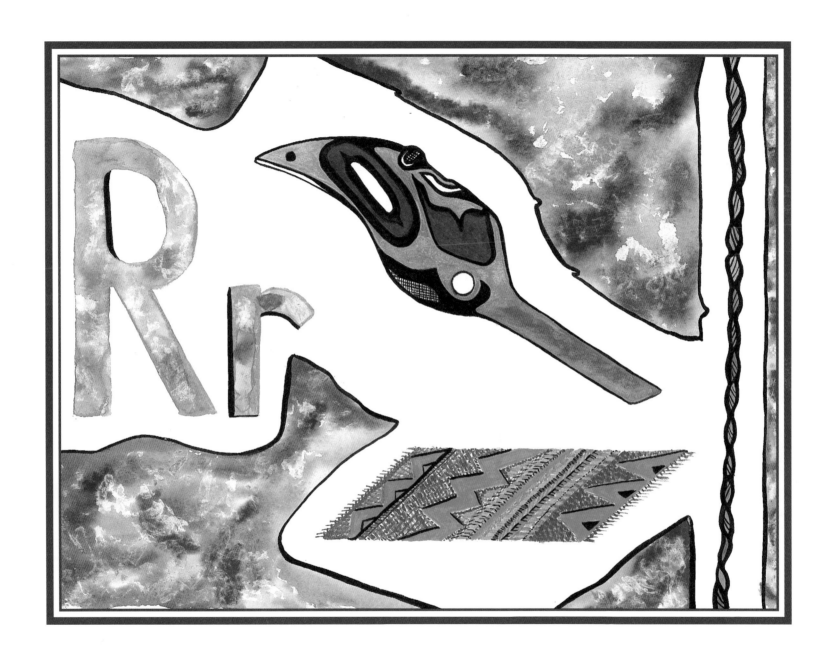

S s is for Sweat Lodge.

Many First Nations have the Sweat Lodge. It is a Purifying Ceremony. Sometimes we fast for a few days before we enter the Sweat Lodge. We pray and meditate, we ask the Creator to be with us and guide us so we can make the right choices in life.
Sage Smudging is a cleansing wash and prayer in the smoke of burning Sage.

snow shoes   sunshine
Sweat Lodge   Sage Smudging

Tt is for Tepee.

The tepee is more than a shelter, it stands for the Values and Ethics we want in our homes. The poles meanings are; Respect, Happiness, Love, Family, Strength, Gratefulness, Humility Sharing, Gentleness, Hope, Protection, Creator's Guidance and Happy Children. From Longhouse to tepee we all have family values. First Nation's Teachers are very important in our modern society.

Thunderbird   tepee   teacher

Uu is for Universe!

There are many First Nations that have stories and legends about "Sky People". Some of the stories tell about gifts that are given to us by People from the sky. Others tell about First Nation's people living with "Sky People" and returning with Spiritual Guidance. There are also legends about "Sky People" coming to earth and staying with us. Respect the Universe as we do.

Vv is for Vision Quest.

The Vision Quest is an experience that helps you understand your personal relationship with the Creator. You fast for a couple of days, which prepares you to be with the Creator. You give yourself because you are the only thing you can give. Not eating is easy, because you're giving all you have to the Creator. Then you find a safe, isolated, special part of Mother Earth, and you spend the night in a "Sacred Circle" praying for Guidance.

Ww  is for Water.

Water is the giver of all life on earth. May we respect and care for this sacred gift. When you use water it is best if you give thanks for it.

Wind   Waves   Weaving

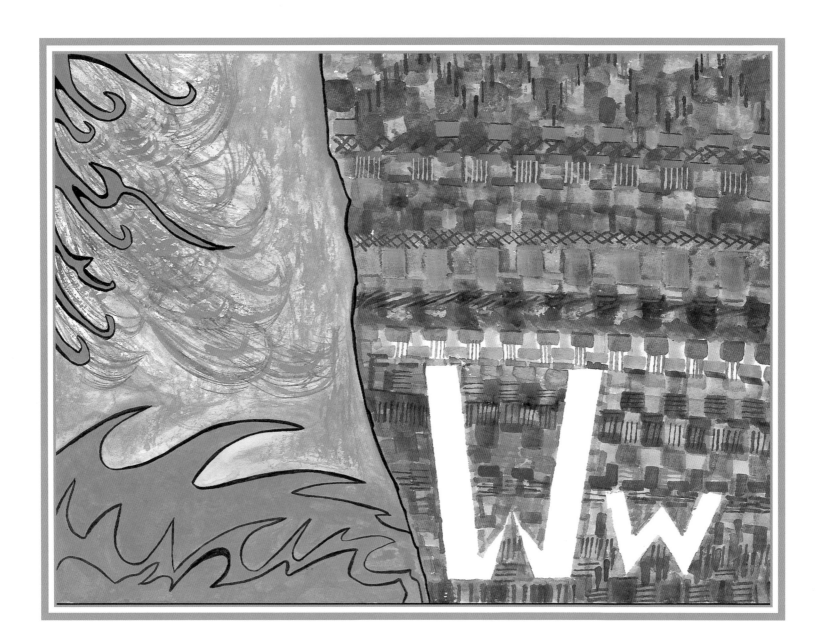

Xx is for Kisses!

Make sure you get a XXXXXXXX from your Mom before you go to bed every night!

XXXX   XXXX   XXXX   XXXX
XXXX   XXXX   XXXX   XXXX

Yy & Zz

stand for The Yakima Nation and The Zuni Nation.

Throughout North America there are over a thousand First Nations. Our Languages, traditions, Art, and homes are unique and distinct yet, we do share many Spiritual Values and Prayers. The Yakima Nation is now in the state of Washington, The Zuni in the Southwest states.

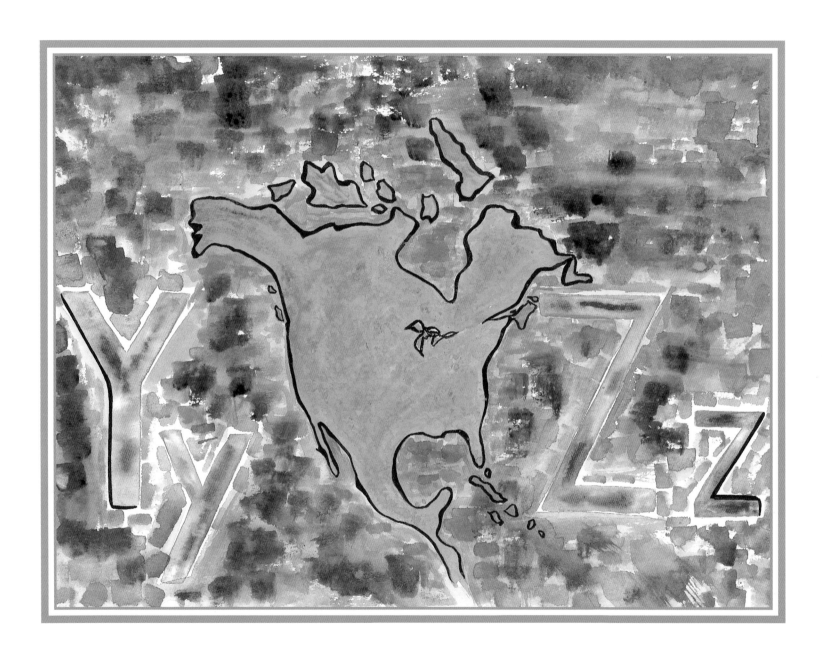

Extended Activities

Aa   Make your own ABC book! You could use different themes such as:
Food, favourite toys or animals.

Bb   Find out how a "Northwest Coast" bentbox is made. Make some bannock.

Cc   Examine all the ways the cedar tree is used.

Dd   Make a drum out of a coffee can and stretched leather.

Ee   Write a short Prayer and try to remember it for the next time you see an Eagle.

Ff   Have a Feast.

Gg   Create your own game.

Hh   Use hoola hoops and learn how to Hoop Dance.

Ii   Carve an animal out of ivory soap.

Jj   Use beads and shells and create some jewellery.

Kk   Draw a killerwhale in "Northwest Coast" style, using ovoids,
"U" shapes, and "S"shapes.

Ll   Visit a First Nation Lawyer.

Mm Make a Medicine Bundle. Be sure to put some Sage or Sweet Grass in your bundle. Wear it close to your heart.

Nn Find a natural field, take off your shoes and go for a walk. Feel the air, touch the surrounding trees and listen to sounds of Nature.

Oo Go to the library and find a book about Ogopogo.

Pp Make some pemmican. Dried crushed berries and dried bits of smoked meat.

Qq Draw a star pattern using a diamond shape, colour it in your favorite colours.

Rr Find different designs in First Nation's rug weaving and try to draw them.

Ss Smudge in some sage, while saying a little prayer.

Tt Read a legend about the Thunderbird and Killerwhale.

Uu Look up in the sky when the stars are shining bright, and find the Milky Way.

Vv Fast for a day or two and take time to be by yourself... outdoors. Say a Thankyou Prayer, and a Guidance Prayer to be a good person.

Ww When it's windy but safe go out and feel the wind in your face.

Xx Give your Parents a hug tonight.

Yy & Zz Find out all you can about the Yakima and Zuni Nations.

A Sweetgrass Prayer

Creator, maker of all that is good

I wash my eyes to see
the beauty in all of creation

I wash my mouth so that I
choose my words with care

I wash my hands to create
and be gentle

I wash my legs so they'll be
strong to carry me through life

and I wash my heart to be kind,
loving and forgiving

all my relations.

Kim Soo Goodtrack is of mixed heritage. Her mother's family is from the Woodmountain Indian Reserve in Saskatchewan.

Kim has attended the University of Guelph and graduated with a degree and professional teaching. certificate from Simon Fraser University. She has worked as Native Indian Cultural Enrichment Officer and Teacher for the Vancouver School Board. As an artist, Kim has also exhibited her visual abstract paintings in Vancouver, Richmond and Toronto galleries.